Other Orca Soundings
by Lesley Choyce

Refuge Cove (2002)
Thunderbowl (2004)
Wave Warrior (2007)
Running the Risk (2009)
Reaction (2010)
Breaking Point (2012)
Rat (2012)
Crash (2013)
Off the Grid (2015)
Scam (2016)

Identify

Lesley Choyce

orca soundings

ORCA BOOK PUBLISHERS

Library and Archives Canada Cataloguing in Publication

Choyce, Lesley, 1951–, author
Identify / Lesley Choyce.
(Orca soundings)

Issued in print and electronic formats.
ISBN 978-1-4598-1406-6 (paperback).—ISBN 978-1-4598-1407-3 (pdf).—
ISBN 978-1-4598-1408-0 (epub)

I. Title. II. Series: Orca soundings
PS8555.H668134 2017   jC813'.54   C2016-904580-3
C2016-904581-1

First published in the United States, 2017
Library of Congress Control Number: 2016950085

Summary: In this high-interest novel for teen readers, Ethan's new friend
Gabe is being harassed for being different than all the other girls.

RECYCLED
Paper made from
recycled material
FSC® C103567
www.fsc.org

*Orca Book Publishers is dedicated to preserving the environment and has
printed this book on Forest Stewardship Council® certified paper.*

Orca Book Publishers gratefully acknowledges the support for its
publishing programs provided by the following agencies: the Government
of Canada through the Canada Book Fund and the Canada Council
for the Arts, and the Province of British Columbia through
the BC Arts Council and the Book Publishing Tax Credit.

Cover image by iStock.com

ORCA BOOK PUBLISHERS
www.orcabook.com

Printed and bound in Canada.

20 19 18 17 • 4 3 2 1

Chapter One

It was one of those days. School was just school, but I couldn't take it anymore. I felt the anxiety creeping up inside me. I couldn't breathe. If somebody looked at me the wrong way I was going to scream. I felt scared, and I was angry too. Angry at myself because I couldn't control it. When the bell rang at the end of math, I headed for the back door of the school and ran. I was looking for a place to hide.

There were other kids out and about. I slipped between two parked buses but bumped into Josh and Derek. Those two guys had been on my case since I was twelve. Josh was just lighting up a joint. They both looked at me, saw the freaked-out look on my face, I guess, and laughed. I pushed past them and started to run.

I sprinted across the parking lot, but it felt like my legs were going to give out. So I tucked into a space between two green dumpsters and fell on the ground. It was smelly there, and there was trash scattered all around me, but it was a good place to hide. The lid on one of the dumpsters was open and flipped back, creating a roof for me. I sat there in my own little trashy cave and put my hands over my head. I started rocking back and forth like I do sometimes in my bedroom when everything seems too overwhelming. I sat there and felt the full panicky explosion in my brain overwhelm me. I thought maybe I was going to have a heart attack, my heart was beating so fast.

I stayed like that, my eyes tightly closed, for maybe five full minutes. I heard the bell ring and knew I should go to my next class, but I just couldn't do it. I couldn't face going back into that building. Not now. Maybe not ever again.

When I opened my eyes, someone was standing there looking down at me. At first I didn't know if it was a guy or a girl. But when we made eye contact, eyes soft and sad, I was pretty sure it was a girl. But she had really short hair and was wearing boy's jeans and a flannel shirt. She was wearing earbuds, and I could hear music blaring, but my heart was still beating so loudly,

3

the blood pounding in my ears, it was hard to tell what kind.

I must have looked pathetic. I had really wanted to be alone, but I suddenly felt less crazy as she knelt down beside me. She gently pulled my hands from my head and put the earbuds into my ears. The music poured in like liquid and seemed to push out all my crazy thoughts. I closed my eyes again and just listened.

There was an orchestra and a guy singing like he was in a choir. Somehow he was taking me to some safe and peaceful place. And somehow this person standing here in front of me and I were connected. And not just by these thin little wires. Really connected.

I didn't move until the song was over. Then the girl took the earbuds out and tucked them in her shirt pocket.

We hadn't even spoken yet. But we'd been spotted.

Suddenly Josh and Derek were looking at us. They started banging on the metal lid. The sound was loud and frightening. Josh was laughing now. Pointing and laughing. "What are you two freaks doing?" Derek said. "Having a weirdo convention or what?"

Derek banged on the metal lid some more, and I felt the panic rising again.

Chapter Two

The girl looked at the two creeps, held up her middle finger, then told them to frig off. That was the term she used. "Frig off," she said. "Leave us alone."

They banged some more on our roof, said some pretty rude things to her, but then turned and walked away. The girl looked back at me and touched my shoulder. "You gonna be okay?"

"I doubt it," I said. "I'm a pessimist by nature. I don't ever expect things to get better. I just expect things to get worse. And they usually do."

She smiled a sad smile.

"How come you stopped and shared your music?" I asked.

"Looked like you needed it. I use the music to drown out things around me."

"Thanks."

"No problem. You're Ethan, right?"

"Yeah. We were in English together last year, weren't we?"

"I sat over by the windows," she said, "and didn't participate much."

"Yeah," I said. "I sat in the back and tried to be invisible."

"You did a pretty good job of it. But I saw you."

I remembered. She had looked different then, with longer hair, different clothes.

"Gabriella, right?" I asked.

"Gabe. Only my mother calls me Gabriella and only when she's mad."

"How often is that?"

"Often."

I smiled. "I can relate." When our eyes met this time, she looked away.

To break the awkward silence I said, "Hey, thanks."

"You already said that."

"Oh, yeah." Another few seconds of dead air.

"C'mon," Gabe said finally. "I don't think you should be going back to class right now."

She got up and walked out from between the two dumpsters, then held out her hand and tugged me back out into the sunlight.

I followed as she began walking away from the school. I knew I'd get shit from my parents for skipping classes again. They always seemed to find out. But I didn't care. I needed this. And I needed to be with her.

We didn't talk much as we walked for several blocks. Then she led me into a graveyard. It was old and not well taken care of. Nobody had been buried in here for a long time. The gravestones were all old and weathered. Some were cracked, and some had been knocked over by vandals.

"This is my favorite place in town," Gabe said. "It's full of people, but not one of them will give you shit. That's my kind of people."

As she led me through the cemetery, Gabe touched each stone as we passed. I found myself doing the same. I also found myself thinking dark thoughts again. "So you put up with all this crap in life," I heard myself saying out loud, "and then you die and they put you in the ground. And that's it."

Gabe shook her head. "No. You live your life first. You *really* live it. You don't just put up with it."

I felt bad for sounding so negative.

But then she smiled. "And *then* you die and they put you in the ground."

I may have actually smiled myself. Shocking that I remembered how. It had been a really long time.

"Look up," Gabe said. "Up there in those big trees."

I looked up, but I didn't really notice anything. Then Gabe clapped her hands—just once, loudly—and a pair of pigeons took off from the branches. They flew high and then circled around the cemetery.

"I love watching them fly."

"Very cool," I said as the pigeons swooped low, right in front of us, before arcing up again to land back on a branch of one of the big trees. Gabe reached in her pocket and pulled out a handful of cracked corn and threw it on the ground.

"It's like they were showing off," I said. "It's like they know we're watching them."

"You're absolutely right. They do that every time I come here."

"How often is that?" I asked as a couple of pigeons swooped down, landed and started pecking at the corn on the ground.

"Often," she said, looking across the rows of gravestones. "I like to make up imaginary stories about the names I find here."

"Really? Like what?"

"Pick a name."

I pointed to a weather-beaten chunk of granite. "Harold Hinkey," I said. "Born 1904, died 1974."

"Harold Hinkey," she repeated. "He was a banker. A mean banker. Straight-laced, everything by the book. He liked to foreclose on widows and take away their houses if they couldn't keep up with mortgage payments. He was rotten harsh to people, but he was punished for it."

"Punished?" I had been pulled right into Harold's life.

"Well, his first wife died and he remarried not long after. See there, next stone over. Helen Hinkey. She outlived him by ten years. He didn't know it when he married her, but she turned out to be a nasty piece of work. Treated poor Harold like dirt. Ordered him around. Wouldn't let him have an ounce of fun. Maybe old Harold was happy to end up in here and have a little peace." She made a small bow in my direction. "Your turn."

She pointed to another, much less fancy headstone.

"Robert Culper," I said. "Born March 12, 1846, died March 12, 1945. Hey, he died on his birthday!"

"Ninety-nine years old," Gabe noted. "Do you think there is something to that?"

"Hell yes," I said. "He was trying to make it to one hundred! Not many people did back then. He had a bet with an old high school buddy that he'd make it."

"Guess he lost that bet."

"But maybe that's what got him to ninety-nine. It kept him going. Old Robert was an adventurer. Been to Alaska looking for gold. Sailed on an old schooner around the world. Married a beautiful woman he met in Singapore."

"Then why did he settle down in this boring old place?"

"He needed someplace quiet to raise the kids. He had twelve. Twenty grandkids and a whole whack of great-grandkids. And guess what?"

"What?"

"He was happy."

Gabe gave me a really funny look. And it kind of clicked. *How unlike me to make up a happy story.*

"Bor–ing," she said and then gently punched me on my arm.

"What was that song anyway?" I asked.

"What song?"

"The one you were listening to when you gave your earbuds to me."

"Oh, that was 'Bridge Over Troubled Water,' by a couple of old folksingers, Simon and Garfunkel."

"Never heard of them," I said. "But thanks again."

"Stop saying that."

Changing the subject, I said, "You know, I really love this graveyard. And you're right about the crowd here. Beats the hell out of school."

Chapter Three

That time with Gabe in the cemetery really settled me down. As we continued to wander among the gravestones, I found myself trying to come up with a label for the kind of person she was.

"Just wondering," I said. "What's with the new fashion statement?"

As soon as I said the words, I wished I could take them back.

"What do you mean?" she asked sharply.

"Forget it," I said. "It's not important."

She stopped walking. "No. Maybe it is. I dress like this because it makes me feel more like me. Last year I decided to stop dressing all girly like my mom always made me. Like people expected. So I cut off my hair and changed my look. I decided that it was time I controlled my own image."

"And that worked for you? Now you're happy?"

"Happier," she said, smiling.

"Cool."

"Now it's my turn to grill you. You weren't exactly sitting by the trash because you were looking for a quiet place to do your homework. What gives?"

"My mom says I'm just too sensitive. That I'll outgrow it. But I've been like this for a couple of years. I feel overwhelmed by everything. And my

17

parents have been fighting a lot lately. It's always tense at home."

"That sucks. I know what that's like."

"I can't concentrate in school, and my grades are in the toilet. If I can't pull things together, I'll probably be held back this year."

"Been there. Done that."

"But you seem like you have it together now. What's your secret?"

"I don't know. I mostly stopped worrying about what other people thought of me. People like Josh and Derek and Brianna and Skylar. The girls were the worst."

"Yeah, I've seen Skylar trashing a couple of the younger girls. What's her problem?"

"Just mean, I guess. But I don't let her get to me anymore."

"I wish I could do that with the way I feel sometimes. Just say I don't give a shit. But it's not like that for me.

Every day is a new struggle to just hold it together. And every day it feels like I'm losing the battle. You saw me back there. Pretty pathetic."

"You never found something that works when you're feeling really uptight?" she asked, looking concerned.

"Well, sort of. One thing."

I had promised myself I wasn't going to take them today. And that was partly why I had ended up out by the dumpsters. I reached in my pocket and pulled out a small sandwich bag containing a few red pills. "These help," I said.

Gabe looked shocked. "Downers?"

"Yeah. I don't even know exactly what they are, but some kind of downer for sure."

"You get these from your doctor?"

I shook my head. "I get them from some guy."

"Not good, Ethan."

"I know."

Suddenly Gabe looked at her wrist—she was wearing some kind of old-style men's watch like my grandfather used to have. "Oh shit," she said. "I gotta get back to school. I've got a test in final period I can't miss. You wanna go back there with me?"

"No, thanks. I think I'll stay here with the dead people."

"Tomorrow, Ethan, we're gonna get to work on you. The *new* you." She looked me in the eye and then turned and began to run back in the direction of the school.

I stayed there in the cemetery for a bit, but it wasn't the same. Now that I was alone, I felt the old anxiety building back up inside me. I looked at the bag of pills in my hand for a moment, then took out two and swallowed them quickly before I had time to reconsider.

Chapter Four

I should have gone back to school for the last class of the day—world history. I was falling way behind. But instead, I walked the streets for an hour as the downers kicked in and I felt that comfortable fuzziness in my head. When I went home, I discovered my father had left work early. He and my mother were in the kitchen arguing,

21

this time over money. I'd heard it all before, so I crept up the stairs to my room and closed the door.

In the morning, I told myself this day would be different. I'd get to see Gabe again, and I desperately hoped she'd be happy to see me too. As I walked to school, I thought about her in a way I'd never thought about a girl before. The truth is, I'd never been very good around girls. In fact, most girls kind of scared me. But not Gabe. She was different.

I fingered the bag of pills in my jacket pocket. *Should I or shouldn't I?* I thought about the day before. I had decided in the morning not to take any and to do school completely straight. That hadn't turned out so well. *Okay. Just one.* I popped it in my mouth and swallowed. It kicked in in time to help me drift through English and math. Not stoned or anything. Just kind of detached. There but not there. Between classes I wandered the halls.

I never did find Gabe. Instead, she found me right before lunch.

"Hiding from me?" she said, a little smile on her face.

"Just the opposite. I was looking for you all morning."

She leaned in close to me. "Boy, do you look relaxed. What's with that?"

I just shrugged and gave her a sheepish smile.

"I get it," she said. "But you're going to have to learn to do without your little helpers."

"How do I do that?" I asked.

"Ethan, it's really quite simple. You just have to not give a shit about what anyone thinks of you."

"How?" I asked again.

Gabe scanned the busy hallways. "Watch."

I followed Gabe through a crowd of rowdy kids. I noticed that some of them gave her weird looks, but some of the guys just got out of her way when they saw her coming. She headed for a group of really loudmouthed girls. I knew that one of them was Skylar, notorious as one of the most stuck-up, bitchy girls in the whole school. I didn't know what they were going on about, but they all shut up when Gabe stopped.

"Skylar," Gabe said, "I was wondering if you'd mind if I borrowed your makeup?"

I could tell her tone was sarcastic, but I wasn't sure where she was going with it.

Skylar stared at Gabe in disbelief. The other girls looked equally shocked. Then Skylar went nuts. "Are you out of your mind?" she shouted. "I'm not lending anything to you. How *dare* you ask me something like that?" She gave Gabe a look of pure loathing and then yelled at her again. "Lesbo!" She sputtered something else I couldn't really hear, but I bet it was something vile.

Then Skylar turned and walked away, her posse at her heels.

Gabe just stood there calmly. Half the kids in school had frozen in their tracks to watch the end of the little drama. Gabe raised her voice just slightly as she said to the quickly disappearing Skylar, "I guess I'll take that as a no?"

Gabe walked back over to me, ignoring the stares. "Funny that she called me that," Gabe said to me, her voice still raised. "I don't even like girls." Then she grabbed my arm and walked me down the hall, all eyes still on us.

When I was able to speak again, I asked her, "Where'd you learn how to do that? To control yourself? To not freak out with everyone watching?"

"I taught myself," Gabe said, obviously proud of the ruckus she had caused. "Someone can say or do anything to you, but it's up to *you* how you react."

25

Chapter Five

That afternoon Gabe invited me to her house so we could do our homework together. Her mom was in the kitchen, and Gabe yelled, "I'm home," but she didn't introduce me. "C'mon," she said and led me upstairs to her bedroom. While we were there she turned her back to me and changed her shirt. She did this as if I wasn't even there, as if she wasn't the slightest bit self-conscious. It kind of freaked me out. Then I followed her back downstairs, and we cracked open our textbooks in the living room.

The downer had worn off, and my head was perfectly clear. I felt nervous being alone with Gabe, but I knew she didn't want me to take another pill. We sat side by side on the sofa, and I could feel her warmth beside me. It was so quiet that I could also hear her breathing, and after a while I noticed that my breathing was perfectly in sync with hers. It was more than a little hard to concentrate on my world history text.

But the funny thing was, I did well on the quiz the next day. Without even asking, I walked Gabe home after school, and she started coaching me on math, my weakest subject. She was very patient and walked me through some of the things I had been missing that year at school.

"You have a way of somehow getting it all to make sense. Before, it just seemed like gibberish," I told her.

"Thanks," she replied. "That's good to hear. I think I may want to be a teacher someday. I just don't know if I'd ever get a job or if kids would accept me the way I am."

I didn't really know what she meant by that, but I wanted to. I knew there was a discussion she and I had to have sometime down the road. But I wasn't ready for that yet.

At school I noticed kids looking at us when we walked down the hall together. I didn't know why, but I had taken to wearing flannel shirts and jeans like she did. Whenever someone was rude enough to stare at us, Gabe prompted me to stare right back. I'd pop a downer once in a while, if I was on my own and the old anxiety monster was creeping up on me, but it was much less often. I found myself actually listening in class rather than just drifting through school as if in a dream.

Because of her, my life now seemed to have meaning and purpose. But one part of me still expected it all to shatter. Things were getting worse at my house, and I found myself hanging out at Gabe's house until five or six o' clock before heading home to a burned dinner and screaming parents.

When I was alone with my thoughts, I still thought of her as Gabriella, which seemed liked the sexiest name on the planet, but if I tried calling her that, she always insisted I call her Gabe. I knew I had strong feelings for her, and I couldn't get her out of my head. But I also knew I was confused about many things.

Finally, during one of those quiet after-school study times, I decided to tell her how I felt. "Gabe, I think I'm falling in love with you," I blurted out.

She stopped reading and looked up at me. "Whoa. Slow down, buddy. How many other girls have you ever been close with?"

"None," I admitted.

"My point exactly. Maybe you don't know what love is. Maybe it's just a word you heard."

"And maybe not."

Gabe took a deep breath. "Well, then, maybe you like me because I'm a girl who likes to dress like a boy and act like a boy."

"I don't think you act like a guy."

"But I do. I think more like a guy and act more like a guy. Haven't you noticed?"

Well, I'd noticed she wasn't like other girls, but I just thought she was different. "Oh shit," I blurted out. "Does that mean I'm, like, gay?"

A hint of a smile erased her super-serious look. "No, dork. It just means you're a little confused. Like a lot of us."

"What if I like you, if I have these feelings for you, just because…" For a few seconds I was stumped. I wasn't sure how to end that sentence. "Because you are…well, you."

"Now that makes more sense," she said with a big smile. She leaned toward me, and I almost thought she was going to kiss me. Instead, she made a fist and, ever so gently, knocked on my forehead. "Now let's get back to work," she said.

Chapter Six

When I got home, I found my mom and dad sitting in the living room. They were oddly quiet. Usually I had to tiptoe past them as they argued and slink off to my bedroom. But this time I didn't.

"What's up?" I asked, sitting down on the sofa.

My dad looked at me with a hangdog face and then stared at the rug.

"Your father has lost his job," my mother said.

"They let me go," he said. "It wasn't my fault. Things are just slowing down."

I didn't say what I wanted to say. I knew he had come home early a few times because he'd been caught drinking on the job. My dad had problems. He'd be the first to admit it. But now wasn't the time to bring them up.

"They say there's lots of construction work up north. I'm thinking I should go up there, get a job and then move you guys up as soon as I can find a place."

My mom said nothing, but I could tell by the look on her face that she hated the idea. *I* hated the idea. How could he do this to us? Do this to me? It just wasn't fair.

The silence filled the room. I felt the old anxiety grab my shoulders and squeeze. "I'm not moving," I announced and got up to go to my room.

I sat down on my bed and started writing a text to Gabe. Then I remembered she'd told me she didn't really do texting. She thought people walking around texting looked like zombies. I tried calling her cell phone but only got a message. "Call me, Gabe," I said after the beep. "Please."

She didn't return my call.

After about a half hour of me sitting in my room staring at the wall and trying to fend off my demons, I decided to go back to her house.

Her father answered the door. He looked a little suspicious of me. "Yes?"

"Hi. I'm Gabe's friend from school. Is she home?" I asked.

"Gabriella is in her room," her father answered curtly.

"Could you please tell her I'm here?"

But Gabe was already coming down the stairs.

"Sorry, Ethan," she said. "I don't usually get phone messages. I just noticed you called."

Her dad was still eyeing me suspiciously. Gabe looked at him. "Dad, this is my friend Ethan," she said matter-of-factly. And then, after a pause, "We study together."

"Hi, Ethan," her dad said, maybe a bit reluctantly. "C'mon in."

I followed Gabe into the living room while her father headed into the kitchen. I told her about my dad losing his job and that we might have to move.

"What is it with parents?" she asked. "Why do they have to be in charge of everything? They just don't get it at all." She seemed angry about something too.

"So are we talking about my parents or yours?"

"All parents. By the time you hit sixteen, you should be able to make all your own decisions. You shouldn't have to do what they want."

"Agreed." I could tell that she was really upset, but I also realized it probably wasn't about my situation. "Gabe, what's going on?"

She took a deep breath. "My parents have been getting flak from other parents in the neighborhood."

"About what?"

"About me. They say I'm a bad influence on their younger kids."

"In what way?"

"'Cause I don't look or act like a normal girl."

"That's crazy!"

"Yeah, but it reinforces what my parents have been feeling all along. And I haven't even told them about the hate mail I've been getting. I had to delete my accounts. It was just getting too weird, too nasty. You wouldn't believe the things people write about me."

"Who?"

"I don't even know. Is it really so bad that I don't dress the proper way or act the way I'm supposed to?"

Gabe looked like she was about to cry, and that didn't seem like her at all.

"I'm feeling like maybe there really is something wrong with me," she said. "I agreed to go talk to the minister at my parents' church. I used to go there too, but I stopped a couple of years back. It just wasn't for me."

"What did the minister say?"

"He tried to be nice, but it was really awkward. I'm not sure he even understood why I was there. *I* wasn't so sure why I was there, but I was trying to please my parents. In the end, he just looked at me and said, *You know, Gabriella, God loves us all*. This wasn't exactly what my parents wanted to hear.

In the end, he gave them the name of some frigging teen counselor. So now I have to go do that."

"Don't do it," I told her. "There's nothing wrong with you. In fact, you're the greatest person I ever met."

She smiled. "Thanks for saying that. But I told them I'd go. Just to keep them off my back. Will you go with me?"

"Definitely," I said.

Chapter Seven

When I walked into my house later that night, my mother was sitting at the kitchen table crying.

"What's wrong?" I asked.

"It's your father. He went out tonight. He was drinking. Then he smashed up the car and got arrested for drunk driving."

"Is he okay?"

"I think so. But he's been charged and is being held at the police station."

"We have to go down there, Mom."

"No," she said. "He deserves to be in jail." She sounded really angry now.

"We need to bring him home," I insisted.

At first my mom just sat there. But then she wiped the tears from her eyes, blew her nose and picked up the keys to her car hanging on the wall. Neither of us spoke a word on the ride to the police station.

By the time we arrived, my mom had pulled herself together, and she told me to sit in the waiting room while she talked to the police. As I sat there worrying about my dad, I had my first panic attack in quite a while. I was finding it hard to breathe, and I started shaking. I leaned over and put my head between my knees.

A cop walking through the waiting room saw me. "Hey," he said, sitting down beside me. "You're looking like you're in pretty rough shape. You in trouble?"

I took a gulp of air and straightened up. "Not me. My dad."

"The guy who smashed up his car?"

"That's my dad."

"He was pretty wasted. The good news is, he didn't get anybody killed and he didn't get hurt."

"He lost his job," I offered by way of explanation.

"I did the same damn thing once. Got fired. Got loaded. Got into an accident. It's what we men do."

It seemed really weird that this cop was trying to make me feel better.

"I'm Officer Dave Newton, by the way," he said and stuck out his hand for me to shake. "They call me Do-Good Dave."

"Do-Good Dave?" I said.

"Yep," he said. "Once they tag you with a nickname like that, it sticks. Can I get you a Coke or something?"

"No, thanks."

"You got a name, kid?"

"Ethan."

"Well, Ethan," said Dave, "I gotta go. Your dad's in trouble, but it's not the end of the world. He'll get past it. Just don't let him drink and drive again." Then he handed me a business card, adding, "Take this. If you need to, give me a call."

"Thanks," I said as he got up to go. I sat there, feeling a little better, realizing it was probably the only time in my life I'd ever had a conversation with a cop. I had always expected them to be pushy and cold. This guy wasn't. And I was thankful for it.

My dad looked really bad when my mom finally walked him through to the waiting room. When he saw me, he dropped his eyes and let my mom lead him out of the station.

Once we were home, they got into a really horrible fight. Mom started screaming first. Then he got going. It was loud and it was nasty. I tried to get them to cool down, but then they both started shouting at me, telling me to shut up and go to my room. *Fine*.

In my room, I started to feel that old familiar anxiety as the yelling continued. I opened a drawer and looked at my stash of pills. I really needed something if I was going to make it through the night.

I was holding one in my hand when I heard something smash downstairs. I ran partway down the stairs and saw a lamp in pieces on the floor. Everything had gone really quiet. Then my dad started to cry, and my mom started to as well. I didn't know what to do. I just stood there, watching my family going to pieces. Then I turned and headed back up to my room, popping the pill into my mouth and swallowing.

Chapter Eight

My parents were silent at breakfast. Usually I'd just grab a piece of toast and run out the door. But today I decided to sit down with them. Without asking, my mom shoveled some scrambled eggs onto my plate.

"I'm sorry you had to see me like that," my dad said. "That was really stupid of me. I'm gonna try to make things right."

My mom gave me a weak smile. I didn't even know what he meant by that, but I knew he was a good man. He just had a bad habit of really screwing things up sometimes.

"I'll lose my license," my dad said. "I'll have to go to court. We can't move until after that."

I wanted to remind him that I didn't want to move at all, but I didn't have the nerve to say it out loud again. "I'm gonna hang out with Gabe after school again today," I said. "We're going to do some homework." What I didn't say was that I was actually going with her to see that counselor, something we were both really nervous about. But Gabe had been there when I needed her, so it was the least I could do for her.

"You should really bring her around the house sometime," my dad said. "I'd like to meet her."

"I think we better wait until things settle down around here," said my mom.

I didn't see Gabe until third period. Kids had been looking at me funny all day. I figured they knew about my father and his accident. Leave it to Josh to be the one to say something to my face.

"Ethan, ol' buddy," he said. "I hear your old man got shit-faced and drove the family car into a tree."

Gabe had just found me and was about to come to my defense. But I wanted to show her that I'd learned a few lessons from her. "Thanks for the concern, Josh," I said flatly. "It's much appreciated." Deep down I was rattled, but I wasn't about to show it.

Josh just kind of blinked and seemed truly disappointed he had not gotten to me. Strangely enough, when he realized

I wasn't going to react, he just walked away.

"Good work," Gabe said. "You handled that nicely. What was that about anyway?"

I told her what had happened.

"That's terrible. Has your father done things like that before?"

"Never. I'm really worried."

"Anything I can do to help?" Gabe asked.

"Not really. Just be my friend," I said although *friend* wasn't really the word I meant.

Gabe looked at me with a sad, soft smile. "You still want to go to that counselor with me today?"

"Absolutely. It might even help keep my mind off the trouble at home."

The counselor was a woman in her early thirties who had an office above a coffee shop. She had insisted on seeing Gabe without her parents, but Gabe had convinced her to let me come along. She invited us to call her by her first name, Elizabeth or Liz.

"Gabriella," she said once we were seated, "I'm going to be asking you some pretty personal questions. Are you sure you want Ethan to be part of this?"

"I'm sure," said Gabe. "But please call me Gabe."

"Of course. Well, Gabe, why don't you tell me why you are here."

"Because my parents wanted me to come. I'm doing it for them."

"Yes, I spoke with them, and they expressed concern for you. They want you to be happy."

"I'm sure they do," Gabe said. "But their idea of happy isn't mine. I think if people would just leave me alone, I'd be perfectly fine."

"What do you mean by being left alone?" the counselor asked.

"I mean, no one should tell me how to look or how to act."

"Does it make you angry when people do that?"

"Yeah, it does. I guess that's why I had that big blow-up with my parents. They were treating me like a little kid. They started lecturing me again about how I should dress. It really pissed me off."

"But you agreed to their suggestion for you to come and talk to me."

"I figured it couldn't hurt."

"Well, I'm glad you came."

Gabe just shrugged.

"Why do you think people want you to look and act a certain way?" Liz continued.

Gabe looked over at me, and I could see that she was uneasy. I almost wanted to answer for her.

"Because I'm not like everyone else. And that makes people uncomfortable."

"How do you identify yourself?"

"What do you mean?" Despite her words, I got the feeling Gabe knew exactly what Liz meant.

"You say that you are not like everyone else. So how do you describe yourself?"

"I just describe myself as 'different,'" Gabe answered, crossing her arms and scowling a bit.

"In what way?"

"Look at me."

"I *am* looking at you," Liz replied calmly. "But I would like to know more about how *you* see yourself."

I had to admit, I was grateful that the counselor was being so persistent. I wanted to hear Gabe's answer too.

"Sometimes," Gabe began, and then stopped. She took a deep breath.

"Sometimes I think I'm a boy in a girl's body."

Liz nodded.

"But sometimes," Gabe continued, "I feel like a girl in a girl's body. Especially when I'm with Ethan."

Liz looked over at me with a faint smile. "That's not so unusual," she said. "But do you find that confusing?"

"Sometimes. But isn't everyone a little confused sometimes?"

"Of course."

"Then why can't people, especially my parents, just accept me for who I am?"

"I don't know if I can truly answer that. But tell me this: Do you want to change, for your parents, or for anyone else, so that you can fit in more easily?"

"No, I don't. Is there anything wrong with that?"

"No, there isn't," Liz answered. "And that's a good starting point for our discussions. I wanted to have a better sense of your perspective before we began. And I want you to know that you're not the only one who has feelings like this."

"I know that," said Gabe. "In fact, I've read enough to know that it's way more complicated than what kind of clothes I wear."

"Yes, you're right. Gender identity and gender expression go way beyond male and female," Liz agreed.

"And I know that some people even feel so conflicted about how they were born and who they really want to be that they have an operation to change from one gender to the other."

"Yes, that's referred to as gender reassignment surgery." Liz said. "Have *you* ever thought about that?"

There was a long awkward silence. I felt like a bomb had just exploded.

Gabe just sat there. She turned her head and looked out the window. I couldn't read the look on her face.

After that, Liz kept the conversation light, sticking to everyday, trivial stuff. She tried to draw me in as well, but I was still in shock. When the session was over, Liz walked us to the door and said, "Well, Gabe, I really appreciate your coming in and letting me get to know you. I look forward to talking more with you in the weeks ahead. And thank you, Ethan, for being such a good friend."

Chapter Nine

As we walked out into the afternoon, I was thinking it had been a bad idea to come along. I was in way over my head.

Finally, I just blurted out what I was feeling. "What were you talking about back there? That stuff about surgery and changing from how you were born?"

Gabe stopped walking. "What? You're afraid I'll become more like a guy?"

"I just don't want you to change," I said. I looked around and realized we were just outside the cemetery where Gabe had helped me pull myself together that day.

"But...would you still like me...if I *did* decide to change?"

I didn't know how to answer. I was thinking that if Gabe did something like that—I mean, *surgery*—and it turned out I still liked her...that it might be a bit too weird, a bit too much. But I didn't want to tell her that. Not yet.

She saw my confusion, and she clearly didn't like it. "I'm going to go," she said abruptly. "I'm sorry you came with me today," she added. And then she walked away.

I didn't try to stop her. I knew if I said anything, anything at all right now, it would be the wrong thing.

But I sure as hell didn't want to go home. So I went into the cemetery. Someone had vandalized the place even more since I had been here before. About a dozen old gravestones had been broken in half or knocked over. And then I found an Ethan. It kind of freaked me out. Only the first name was the same, but there it was. *Ethan Clarke, 1840–1856.* Whoever this Ethan was, he had died at sixteen, my age. But even weirder than that were the words beneath the name and date. *We forgive you.*

I sat down right there on the grass. What had he done? Something awful? Killed somebody? Killed himself? Whoever he was, he had been a kid with a problem. A really big problem. "Speak to me, Ethan," I said out loud.

But Ethan had been dead for a long time. He wasn't talking to anyone.

When I got home my dad was sitting at the kitchen table, fussing with his checkbook. "How did the studying go?"

"Fine," I lied.

"This girl, Gabriella. You really should invite her over sometime. We'd like to meet her."

"Sure, Dad," I said. Truth was, I wondered if Gabe would even ever speak to me again. I guess my dad could read something in the way I said it.

"Ethan, you okay?"

I was back to feeling the way I used to feel before I met Gabe. Alone in the world. Afraid. "Sure. I'm okay."

He closed his checkbook. "Look, I'm going to court next week, and I will take my punishment. Then we'll move to a new town and I'll get a good job. We'll start all over. I've explained this to your mother, but she just can't see the light at the end of the tunnel. You'll like it in a new place, right?"

"Right," I said. Maybe I would. Maybe it could never work out between Gabe and me. So hell yeah. Move someplace new where no one knew me. Start all over.

Chapter Ten

I saw Gabe as I was walking into the school. She saw me too. But she just kept walking. I didn't try to catch up to her but hung back and sat down on the low wall out front. When all the other kids had gone in and I felt that old fear creeping up my spine and into my head, I took a couple of my pills. I needed them to get through this day.

I found myself falling into the dreamy state that came with the downers. The tension faded—everything sort of faded. I knew I was slipping back into familiar territory. The school day would drift on by, and me with it. I didn't pay much attention in any class, and walking through the hallways was just noise and a blur of people. It wasn't good, but then, it wasn't as bad as cowering at the back of the school between the dumpsters. I even found myself thinking, Yeah, this all sucks. Leave it all behind when we move and start over again someplace new.

I was on my way to my locker pretty close to the end of the day when I heard someone shouting. I lifted myself out of the fog and went to see what it was all about.

Skylar was shouting. Shouting at Gabe. "Give it up, bitch," Skylar said. "I didn't put anything in your locker. You don't even register on my radar.

I don't care anything about you, so why would I leave you some stupid threat?" I actually thought Skylar was going to hit Gabe, she was so out of control. And Skylar's posse was right there, ready to back her up.

A crowd was forming around them in a circle in that insane way that happens when a fight, especially a girl fight, is about to happen.

I pushed my way through the gawking students and grabbed Gabe by the arm. I could see the anger in her eyes. She was ready to take on Skylar. For exactly what, I didn't know. But I needed to get her out of there quickly.

"Let's go," I said, half pushing her through the mob. I heard Skylar yelling something really crude as we cleared the group and headed toward the sunlight streaming through at the end of the hall.

Outside, Gabe started walking away from me really fast. I went after her and tried to speak to her, but she kept pushing me away. Then she started running. She was fast, and still feeling the effects of the downers, I couldn't keep up.

I watched her, though, and kept walking as fast as I could, hoping she would slow down. Soon she was out of sight, but I kept walking anyway. Eventually I caught up with her. She was sitting in the doorway of an out-of-business bakery. Crying.

Breathing hard, I sat down beside her. The doorway smelled like stale urine. There was garbage on the ground and graffiti on the windows. It was a hellish place. But at least it was just the two of us.

I cautiously touched her shoulder. "What happened?" I asked, but she just shook her head and cried some more.

I touched her hair. "Talk to me. Please."

She reached into her pocket and pulled out a folded-up piece of paper. There was a message on it in big bold letters.

WE'RE GOING TO KILL YOU, FREAK. TAKE THIS AS A WARNING!

"This was in my locker," Gabe said. "I thought maybe Skylar did it."

"We should go to the principal," I said the second I read the words. "This is a death threat. This is *crazy*." Maybe for the first time it was really beginning to sink in for me how difficult life must be for Gabe.

She was still sniffling a bit but pulling herself back together. "No," she said, "it would only complicate things. It would draw more attention to me, and I don't want that. Besides, it's only words." Then she tore up the note and threw the pieces on the ground with the other trash.

"Yeah, but this isn't a joke. This is serious."

"Ethan, people have been posting things online about me for a long time. I stopped paying attention to it. I got off all social media 'cause I was getting hate mail. As long as I didn't read it, it couldn't get to me."

"You thought Skylar was behind it?"

"Maybe some of it. Early on, I could figure out that some of those postings were hers. The wording was unmistakable. But I think I was wrong about this."

"But *someone* did it." I couldn't believe how calm she was about someone threatening to kill her.

"Could be anyone. This kind of shit is easy if you can be anonymous. But like I said, it's only words."

Chapter Eleven

"Let's get out of here," I said.

We stood up and walked in silence for a bit. I was glad the pills were wearing off. My head was getting clear now. Gabe had stopped crying. I told her about the Ethan I had found in the cemetery. She said we should go back there together sometime and check out more gravestones. I said I'd like that.

Then a weird thing happened.

I heard a car coming up behind us and realized it was slowing down. When it was right alongside us, somebody threw something out the window. It hit me in the leg. But it didn't hurt. When I looked down, I saw it was a taped-up cardboard box. The car, an old blue Honda, raced away. I couldn't see the license plate.

Gabe bent over to look at the box, and I grabbed her. "Just leave it," I said. "Don't touch it." I didn't know exactly what I was thinking. Maybe a bomb. Maybe poison or something.

Gabe pulled away from me though. She knelt down to the box and picked it up, then shook it. "Definitely not a bomb," she said.

"Just leave it, Gabe. Get rid of it."

Instead, she ripped the tape off and opened it. She lifted out what was inside. It was a Barbie doll in boys' clothes, with the hair shaved off and a razor blade stuck into its neck.

"What the hell?" I said.

Gabe was visibly shaken. Then she was angry. She threw the box and the doll to the ground. Then she let out the most awful scream I had ever heard. I stood there and didn't move.

A few seconds passed. I could see that she was about to kick the doll into the street.

"Don't," I said. "We need to take this to the police."

Gabe shook her head. "It won't do any good."

I understood what she was thinking. Going to the authorities when bad stuff happened often caused more grief than good. But I was thinking about the cop who had talked to me the day my dad got arrested.

"Trust me on this," I said. "Please."

Gabe stood there, mute, looking hurt and defeated. She watched me as I picked up the doll and put it back in the box. I tucked it under my arm and took her hand. We started walking to the police station.

At the desk inside the station, the clerk in uniform gave us a once-over as we walked in the door. The look on his face said he had already made his mind up about us before we even spoke.

"What can I do for you?" he said.

"I wonder if I can speak to Officer Newton," I said. I could tell Gabe was very uncomfortable.

"You got an appointment?" the man asked.

"No," I said. "But I've got this." I reached into my wallet and showed him the business card. The guy gave me a funny look. Then he leaned over his speaker phone.

"Dave," he said. "You in your office? There's a couple of…um…kids here who want to talk to you."

I couldn't make out the response, but not more than a minute passed before Newton walked into the waiting room. He smiled at me and nodded toward Gabe. Then he looked at the cardboard box in my hands. "C'mon into my office," he said.

We followed him into a small cubicle and sat on two folding chairs. I set the box on his desk and tried to hold Gabe's hand, but she pulled away.

"What do we have here?" he asked.

I opened the box and Newton took a look. I explained what had happened.

"I'm guessing," he said, "that you don't consider this a joke."

I nodded. "There was also a death-threat note in her locker," I added. "And other threats."

"Why didn't you come to us earlier?" he asked Gabe.

She just shrugged.

Newton folded his hands in front of him and looked at Gabe and then me. "I think we should look into this," he said to Gabe. "You gonna be all right?"

Gabe nodded.

Newton asked us some more questions about the other threats and for a description of the car. Gabe explained about the emails and the note in her locker that she had torn up and thrown away.

"Why do you think anyone would want to do this?" he finally asked. But Gabe just shrugged again and didn't answer him.

Chapter Twelve

Officer Newton offered to give us a ride home, but Gabe said no. I knew she was still uncomfortable about getting the police involved, and I was hoping I had done the right thing.

We walked a roundabout route to her house, and I was about to go inside with her, but she stopped me. "I just want to be alone for a while," she said.

I had noticed there was no car in the driveway. That meant that neither her mother nor her father was home.

"I don't think that's such a good idea," I said. "I'm worried about you."

"I'll be okay," Gabe said.

"Are you sure?"

"Yeah, I'm sure."

I didn't like the feel of this. "Hey," I said. "Come to my house. Just for a while, until your parents get home." I had been avoiding having Gabe come to my house because my parents fought so much, and there was always a lot of tension there. But it didn't feel right leaving her alone at a time like this.

She hesitated but then gave in. "Okay. I guess you're right. I don't really want to be alone right now."

When we got to my house, as predicted, I could hear my parents arguing inside. "Oh shit," I said out loud.

Gabe smiled. "It's okay."

I felt embarrassed but was determined to keep Gabe near for as long as I could.

"I'm home," I yelled as we went in the door.

The arguing stopped. "Ethan, is that you?" my mom called.

"Yep."

They both came in from the other room. My mom was still in her housecoat, and my dad had his work pants on and an old, dirty T-shirt. They looked like a couple of slobs, and I felt even more embarrassed.

"This is Gabe," I said.

There was a puzzled look on both their faces, and a few seconds of silence during which I truly hated my parents. Then my stupid father looked at Gabe and said, "Oh, um, hello." I could tell he was about to say more, probably something about how she looked—her clothes, her hair.

My mom could tell, too, and tried her best to shut him up. But not before he added, "I don't get it."

Just like my dad. He rarely did.

"I'd better go," Gabe said, inching back toward the door.

"No," I said. "Please stay." Despite my idiot father and the awkward situation, I didn't want Gabe to be on her own right then.

"Yes," my mom added. "Please stay." My dad nodded his head then, afraid to add anything further lest he get himself into more hot water.

I led Gabe down to the rec room in the basement, where we had a pool table. "I'm not very good at this, but do you want to play?"

"What, no homework today?"

"No. I think we could just hang out."

"Hang out it is," Gabe said, picking up a pool cue and taking the first shot.

It turned out she was a pretty good pool player, and she ended up teaching me a few things about the game. After some time I found myself feeling really relaxed, despite the day's events and the fact that the pills had worn off.

Gabe beat me three games in a row, but it didn't matter because I was just happy she was here.

"You're good for me," I heard myself blurt out at one point. "You know that?"

"And you're good for me, Ethan. You're also good *to* me." Gabe smiled. She had a beautiful smile, one I hadn't seen very often in the short time I'd known her.

Just then I heard the upstairs door open. "Ethan," my mom yelled down, "tell your friend we want her to stay for dinner."

Gabe shook her head no, but I shouted back, "Sure, Mom. What are we having?"

"Lasagna. It has meat in it. I hope she's not a vegetarian."

I looked at Gabe again, and she was still shaking her head no.

"No, she's not a vegetarian. *Ow*!" Gabe had punched me in the arm.

"Good," my mom said, and I heard her close the door.

"I meant *no*," Gabe told me with a stern look. "As in, *no, I don't want to stay for dinner*."

"But you're not a vegetarian, right?"

"Right."

"Then no excuses."

Chapter Thirteen

I was expecting the dinner to be uncomfortable, and it was.

My mom tried to ask Gabe questions about herself and her family and only got one- or two-word answers. My dad kept giving her weird looks. I knew he was trying to figure her out.

"I'm sorry the lasagna is a little overdone," my mom said. She wasn't a very good cook.

"It's perfect," my dad countered. "Ethan's mother is a fabulous cook." I guessed my dad was trying to be on his best behavior.

"Anything interesting happen today for you two?" my mom asked.

Without looking up, I gave my usual answer to this traditional question. "Not really."

"That's funny," my dad said. "Because we had a phone call from a police officer a few minutes ago. He wanted to talk to you, Ethan."

Oh shit, I thought. This is not good.

My dad saw the look on my face. "Don't worry. I asked if you were in some kind of trouble, and he said no. It just seemed a little funny. Do you know what it could be about, Ethan?"

I looked at Gabe. I really didn't want to get into it.

Gabe stopped eating and took a deep breath. Then, to my great surprise, she started telling them about the death threat at school and the box with the doll. She finished by saying, "But Ethan has been there for me every step of the way. He was the one who insisted I go to the police."

My father looked stunned. "That's terrible," he said. "Why would anyone do that stuff to you?" I could tell he was deeply disturbed.

Gabe shrugged. "I guess it's because I'm, well, different. The way I look, the way I act."

Gabe had my father's full attention now. I could see that it was ever so slowly starting to sink in. I expected him to say something really stupid. Instead, he said, "They can't do that to you. It's not right."

"Maybe I'll just have to get used to it," Gabe said. "Maybe I already have."

"No, you shouldn't have to put up with that. No one should. I had an uncle. Stuff like that was happening to him because he was different. I guess today you'd say he was gay."

"What did he do about it?"

I'd heard the stories about Uncle Trevor before. My father always got really angry and upset when he talked about what had happened to Trevor. He had been hounded and taunted his entire school life and had eventually committed suicide. My dad had never gotten over it.

He looked at me, and for a second I thought he could read my mind. He put his fork down and said, "You're welcome to stay for a bit after dinner, Gabe. Whenever you're ready, I'll give you a ride home."

Gabe just nodded, but I could tell from her face that she and my dad had connected for a moment. It was a side of my father I hadn't seen in a long time.

Gabe did stay for an hour or so, and we played some more pool. "I like your parents," Gabe told me at one point. "They're really cool."

"I don't think anyone has ever said that to me in my entire life."

"Well, someone just did."

When we went back upstairs, my mom said she'd take Gabe home. My dad was standing there with a sheepish look on his face. He didn't have to say anything, but he did anyway. "I forgot I lost my license," he told Gabe. "I was bad." He looked and sounded like a guilty little kid.

And then Gabe did the most unexpected thing. She walked over to my dad and gave him a hug.

Chapter Fourteen

The next day was Saturday. I called Officer Newton on his cell phone to see if anything new had come up. "No," he said, "nothing new, and I'm sorry about calling your house and speaking to your dad. I hope it didn't cause you any grief with your parents."

I told him about the dinner conversation, even the part about Uncle Trevor.

"It's a familiar story," he said. "Sad but true. How well do you know Gabe?"

"I think I know her pretty well. She's strong."

Office Newton paused for a moment and then said, "Sometimes people act strong. But then sometimes, when the harassment continues, it becomes too much for them."

"What should I do then?"

"Be there for her. And see if you can figure out who's giving her a hard time. Call me if you need me."

I promised I would, but as I hung up I felt a new kind of panic building inside me. I felt the weight of the responsibility that had been placed on me, that I'd placed on myself. And I wasn't sure if I could handle it.

I couldn't reach Gabe all day. I dropped by her house twice and again on Sunday, but no one was home. When Monday morning rolled around, I was afraid something bad had happened.

On my way to school I swallowed one of the pills. I needed some help to get through the day. By the time I got there, I was feeling a little more relaxed, with a mild fog rolling through my brain.

I waited by room 303, Gabe's first class of the day. When the bell rang she still hadn't shown up. *Damn.*

I thought about calling Officer Newton again. I sat down on the floor of the hallway and just stared at my phone, trying to decide what to do.

I tried calling Gabe again. This time she answered.

"Gabe! Are you okay?"

"Yes. But Ethan, I think you need to keep your distance from me. I want you to leave me alone."

"What happened? Where are you?"

"I'm sorry. I just want you to stop trying to help me. I'm dragging you into something that is my problem, not yours. And your helping…well, that just seems to complicate things."

I didn't understand why she was suddenly pushing me away. "But I *want* to help you."

"Just back off," Gabe said and then hung up.

I tried calling back, but she didn't answer. I reached in my pocket. I needed just one more pill if I was going to make it through today. The fog increased ever so slightly, but enough to drown out the confusion swirling around in my brain.

I survived the day without losing it, but as the drug started to wear off, I decided I had to see Gabe. I walked to her house and saw a car in the driveway. Her mother answered the door. She'd only met me once before.

"You're Ethan, right?"

"Yes. Can I see Gabe?"

"Gabriella doesn't want to see you. We're keeping her home from school for a while. She told us what happened. And I know you've been trying to be helpful, but her father and I think you should stay out of it. We want to handle this our way."

I couldn't figure out what had changed since Gabe came to my house for dinner. It didn't make any sense.

"Is she okay?" I asked.

"She's here, and she's safe. That's all that matters."

"Why can't I see her?"

"I'm sorry. Goodbye." And she closed the door in my face.

That night, sitting in my bedroom, I felt sadder and more alone than I'd ever felt in my life. I was sure I was losing Gabe, losing her one way or another.

In the morning, when she didn't show up at school again, I went looking for her. No one answered the door at her house. At first I thought she might be hiding in her room. I tried the door, but it was locked. I checked the back door and even the first-floor windows, but they were all locked as well. I considered breaking in but immediately realized that was a stupid idea.

I almost took one of the pills in my pocket to ease my nervousness. But I decided this day was going to be different. If I was going to figure out a way to help Gabe, I needed a clear head. To help me stay strong, I dropped the bag in the first garbage can I came across. Something felt very right about that.

I headed for the only place I thought Gabe might be if she wasn't hiding out in her room.

I swung open the gate to the old cemetery and walked in. It was a cool morning, and there was dew on the green grass and on the gravestones.

I spotted Gabe far in the back, sitting beneath a giant oak tree. She was wearing a backpack. She watched me walking toward her. She looked very, very sad.

"Hey," I said, sitting down on the ground beside her.

"Hey. How'd you know I'd be here?"

"I tried your house and no one was home."

"My parents think I'm in school. They dropped me off there, but I didn't go in."

"I came by yesterday too. Did your mom tell you?"

"No, she didn't. But they're both acting really weird now."

I wanted to know why Gabe had stopped talking to me. I wanted to know what had changed.

"They say I shouldn't trust anyone, Ethan. Even you. They took me to see that counselor again. I like talking to her, but my parents don't think she's helping me any. My mom's suggesting I change schools. And maybe that we should move."

"That's insane. You can't just run away like that."

"Something else happened."

"Tell me."

Gabe took off her backpack and slowly opened it up. She took out something wrapped in a small towel. A dead pigeon. I didn't understand.

"This was in our mailbox. Someone killed it and put it there."

"I'm so sorry. Why would anyone do that?"

"It's another threat. But it means more. It also means someone has been watching me. Watching us."

I remembered the other day, when Gabe had brought me to the cemetery.

How she'd shown me the pigeons flying overhead and then fed corn to them.

Gabe looked down at the dead bird. "Sometimes I hate this town and the people in it," she said. "And sometimes I hate my life."

Chapter Fifteen

I found some branches on the ground and we used them to dig a grave for the pigeon beneath the big trees at the back of the graveyard. Gabe let me hold her after that, but I still had the feeling I was losing her. I was sure something bad was going to happen. But I didn't know what to do.

That's when I realized we were being watched. Gabe had her eyes closed, and she might have been crying, because I could feel her body shaking a little. As I held her, I looked up and saw the car. The same old blue Honda of the Barbie-doll incident. And near the car, just outside the fence, I saw a guy smoking a cigarette.

Without saying anything to Gabe, I jumped up and ran across the cemetery toward the gate. The guy saw me and ran for his car. As he was climbing in, I got a pretty good look at him. He was older, but someone who went to my school. I didn't know his name, but I was sure I'd seen him in the halls. So this was the creep harassing Gabe.

I made it to the gate just as the car sped off. I caught the license plate this time, but I still ran like hell as the car sped away. The car turned at the corner, but I wasn't about to give up. I ran across someone's lawn and into their backyard and then through someone else's front yard and out onto the next street. I could see the car at a red light half a block away.

"Please, light. Stay red," I said, still running.

The light listened. It stayed red, and the guy in the Honda didn't see me. I ran up from behind and yanked open the passenger door. I got in.

I could barely breathe and didn't really have a plan for what to do next. The guy was totally freaked out. "Get the hell out of my car!" he screamed. I knew any second he was going to punch me in the face. I wasn't much of a fighter, and I was totally out of my element.

"Yeah, I'll get out," I said, grabbing the keys from the ignition and jumping back onto the street. I heaved his keys as far as I could into some bushes. Then I tried to get control of my breathing. There just wasn't enough air to fill my lungs.

I stood there and watched in slow motion as the guy got out of his car, looking shocked and angry. He was clenching and unclenching his fists as he walked around the front of his car and toward me. The light had changed, and now other drivers were honking their horns. One car started to drive around the Honda and nearly smashed into an oncoming car. Both drivers pounded hard on their horns and shouted at us. But no one was getting out of their cars to get involved.

This guy was one mean, ugly character. The look on his face scared the shit out of me, but I didn't run. Some people across the street had stopped and were staring at us. Honda Guy noticed them watching. He gave me the finger and said, "This isn't over, pissant." And he went searching for his keys.

That's when I saw Gabe running up the street toward us. I didn't want her anywhere near this creep, so I started running toward her.

Halfway down the block I met up with her. Drivers were still blowing their horns at the Honda parked in the road.

"You okay?" Gabe asked.

"I'm perfect," I said, trying to get my adrenaline in check. "Just trying to teach an asshole a lesson." That line was so unlike anything I'd ever said before.

Gabe looked at me and then over at the guy in the bushes. She had a funny look on her face.

"What is it?" I asked.

"I know who that is," she said.

"You *know* him?"

"Not really. I guess I don't know him at all. But I know who he is."

"I've seen him at school, but I don't know his name."

"Tyler," she said with contempt in her voice. "Tyler Macey. He's a senior. A few years ago he came on to me. I was only thirteen at the time. I was flattered. He was older and he was a jock, and I was so young. But he quickly became pushy. Really pushy."

We both watched as Tyler found his keys and headed back to his car. Before he got in, he looked over at the two of us and shook his fist. "What a jerk," I said.

"It wasn't long after he came on to me," Gabe said, "that I decided to change my look. Maybe at first I thought it was to avoid attracting creepy guys like that. But then I decided I liked my new look. It just helped me feel more at home in my body. I know that sounds crazy, but it helped me feel more like who I really was. And as a bonus, guys like Tyler stopped hitting on me."

Chapter Sixteen

I tried to convince Gabe we should go back to the police. At first she resisted, so we just walked around for a bit. Cooling down, I guess you'd say.

Finally, after maybe twenty minutes, Gabe stopped walking and said, "Ethan, I appreciate that you're trying to help me. I really do. I just have a feeling this sort of thing won't go away. If it's not Tyler, it will be someone else."

"If it is someone else, we'll nail him too. Let's talk to the police. The guy we spoke to before."

Something was different when we walked into the police station this time. Officer Newton was in his office. He was just getting off the phone, and he looked really rattled. But he waved us in.

I explained about the dead pigeon and about Tyler watching us in the cemetery. Gabe told him about the incident a few years earlier and how she'd had to forcibly push Tyler away.

Officer Newton looked really uncomfortable now, not at all like the jovial guy I had met the night my dad got arrested. "I appreciate hearing all of this," he said. "However, I just got off the phone with another officer here, and we have a bit of a problem." Gabe and I looked at each other. "This Tyler Macey you're talking about came in here about half an hour ago to file a complaint."

"A complaint about what?"

Officer Newton nodded at me. "You, Ethan. He said you attacked him. That you jumped into his car and started beating on him and then threw his car keys away."

This caught both Gabe and me so off guard that neither of us could speak.

"But I told you what really happened," I offered in my defense. "And I never beat on him, although I sure would have loved to."

Officer Newton put his hands in the air and shook his head. "I'm sorry. He's pressing charges. We have to look into this."

"You're not going to arrest Ethan, are you?" Gabe asked.

Officer Newton seemed really uncomfortable now. "Not exactly," he said and then turned to me. "But we will have to take a statement from you and have your parents come pick you up."

"What about the note in my locker?" Gabe asked. "What about the doll and the dead pigeon? Why can't you charge Tyler? Isn't he the criminal here?"

Newton pursed his lips and then took a deep breath. "I told my supervisor about the note and the doll, and he spoke with our prosecutor. They both said there is no real evidence it was Tyler. I feel bad, but there's no way we can prove that he's the one who did it."

"But we *know* it was him," I said.

"It's your word against his," Newton said. "Just like the car incident."

A female officer took a recorded statement from Gabe in a separate room while Officer Newton recorded my version of the day's events in his office.

When my mom and dad showed up together, my mom hugged me and asked if I was okay. My dad seemed more concerned about Gabe. "What about you?" he asked her. "Are you all right? You're not hurt, are you?"

"I'm fine," she told him. "Please, just get us out of here."

In the car, I did all the talking, explaining what had happened. My mom just looked straight ahead at the road as she drove. My dad kept repeating, "It's just not right."

Chapter Seventeen

The next day Officer Newton called me on my phone and told me the charges against me had been dropped. "I'm not supposed to say anything, but I'm really sorry about the way this played out. It's not the first time I've seen things get switched around by someone who knows how to work the system."

"What if there's another threat?" I asked.

"Then call me. The door's not closed on this. We just need evidence."

"Thanks," I said and hung up.

But I was worried about Gabe, really worried. Now she was more vulnerable than ever. It seemed like anyone could get away with being mean to her as long as they remained anonymous or they didn't get caught in the act.

She didn't go to school for two more days. I called her a few times and we talked, but she said she didn't want me to come over. She said she needed time to think.

"To think about what?" I asked.

"Everything."

"Are you going to be okay?"

"I think so," Gabe said. "It's just that I don't feel safe anywhere but here in my bedroom. And I'm not even 100 percent sure about that."

Identify

It was so weird to hear her say that. That was what I used to feel. Only I'd never really had a reason to feel that way. But I knew exactly what she meant.

People noticed that Gabe wasn't in school, I guess, because kids started asking me about her. Even one of Skylar's friends, Jenna, asked about her. And then she asked, "What really happened?"

"What do you mean?"

Jenna actually seemed concerned. "What really happened with Tyler? He told his buddies some crazy story about you and Gabe. What was that all about?"

So I told her everything. About the doll and the dead pigeon. About how Tyler had treated Gabe when she was younger. I was really shocked to see that Jenna seemed so interested. This was a girl who had never spoken to me in all the years we'd been in school together.

Almost an entire school week had gone by, and Gabe had not left her house. But then, early Friday morning, my cell phone buzzed. I had a text message. Not from Gabe but from her mom.

I'm driving Gabriella to school today. Can we pick you up too? 8:15

I texted back right away. **Absolutely**

When they arrived, I got in the car. Although Gabe's mom tried to sound cheerful, it was clear Gabe was anything but.

"Ethan, please watch out for her today, okay?" her mom said.

"I will," I promised.

Gabe scowled at her mom and then turned around and gave me a look that said she didn't want anything to do with me. I didn't get it. What was going on? I was only trying to help someone I cared a lot about.

At school Gabe told me to just leave her alone. "I can take care of myself," she said. "I'll work through this."

But I kept watch. I guess I sort of stalked her through the day, keeping my distance but making sure she was okay.

Toward the end of the day, I went looking for her and froze in my tracks. I was totally shocked. She was standing outside the chemistry lab, talking with Skylar. They seemed to be having a very serious conversation. Skylar looked concerned and appeared to be asking Gabe all kinds of questions. I decided to hang back and wait to see what happened. Just in case things went bad.

But nothing happened. They both just walked away—together. I tried to read the look on Gabe's face, but I was too far away. I went to my last class of the day, feeling like something, I didn't know what, had shifted.

And something had.

Gabe found me when the final bell rang. "C'mon," she said. "My mom will be waiting to give me a ride home. You want to come over to do some homework?" She had a funny little smile on. At least, I thought it was a smile.

I didn't ask her anything on the drive home, and her mom rattled on as she drove. Something about shopping and traffic.

When Gabe and I were alone in her living room, I asked her, "What was going on with you and Skylar? The last time I saw you two have a 'conversation,' she was screaming at you."

Now Gabe gave me the full 100-watt smile. "Oh, that," she said.

"Well?"

"Well, she was telling me that a while back Tyler had come on to her. At first she kind of liked him. But then he turned really creepy. She brushed him off, and so he started spreading rumors about her. About what they'd done together. Except the stuff wasn't true."

"Nice guy, ol' Tyler Macey," I said.

"She said she's been waiting for a good opportunity to get back at him. She asked me if I minded if she got word out about what Tyler's been doing to me."

"And you said?"

"I said *hell no*."

I've never been a fan of gossip, or of social media in general, for that matter. But when a girl like Skylar decides to use all the technology at her disposal to get back at a guy, it's hard not to stand back and admire the chaos that unfolds.

Skylar told Gabe's story in every way she could. And no matter how much Tyler tried to deny it, the story stuck to him like glue. The note in the locker, the doll, the dead pigeon. And more.

Let's just say Gabe didn't need a court order to stop further harassment. And she soon went back to being her old self. She didn't change her look. In fact, I started seeing more girls cutting their hair real short like hers and wearing flannel shirts. The truth was, she now had a certain amount of status at school.

And maybe I did too. Because everyone knew now that I was Gabe's good…friend…or whatever. And that I had stuck with her through her ordeal.

My dad kept asking me about Gabe and insisted she come over for dinner more often. And she did. One night he even challenged her to a game of pool, and she accepted. I got stuck helping Mom with the dishes.

It was really weird to hear them laughing down there. But a good weird. While I was drying, my mom said, "Your father decided that he doesn't want to have us move away for work after all. He took a job as a janitor at the elementary school."

"Are you kidding?" I asked. This was a real step down from his previous job in construction. I just couldn't picture him mopping floors.

"It was his decision. He says he'll work his way up. Probably get a better job down the line but that it's what he wants to do for now. I'm going to take on some part-time work as well. At least we won't have to move."

For a while Tyler turned his attention to me. He'd stop me outside school or in the hall and tell me he was going to beat the living crap out of me. Once, he said, *I'll get you when you least expect it, and no one is going to know.* He had other well-rehearsed lines too. And he liked to intimidate me by knocking hard into me in the hall or punching me in the shoulder, punching hard and pretending he was just goofing around.

But then his buddies turfed him out of whatever little club they had. So he was forced to hang out with younger guys—Josh and Derek in particular. By then most kids in school saw Tyler for what he really was. Not long afterward he got caught vandalizing a teacher's car. The police were called, and he was forced to pay for the damages. I think the cops had his number from then on.

Gabe made several more visits to the counselor. She came out of there with all kinds of information about gender identity and sexuality, stuff that made my head spin. But one day Gabe announced that she was done with counseling.

"Why?" I asked. "Seems like it's been pretty helpful."

"It has, but things have changed for me. I think I've finally figured something out."

"Really?" I asked.

"Yeah, really," Gabe said. "I may be different, but I feel stronger now. I know that you care about me and like me as I am. That's a part of what makes me stronger. But the most important thing is that *I* like me as I am. And even when things get messy, that's enough."

Her words made a lot of sense. I knew deep down that I wanted to find that inner peace too. I had tried a couple of times to stop taking the pills cold turkey, but the anxiety had kept creeping back.

"Maybe *you* should try going to a counselor," Gabe suggested.

"Maybe," I answered. "I'll think about it." And I meant it. I knew that some things had changed in a big way for me. I was getting stronger too. But the time had come. I had no choice now but to confront my own demons. As someone once said, there's nothing to fear but fear itself. And thanks to Gabe,

I was learning to stop being afraid of fear. I had already stopped caring if anybody laughed at me or tried to hurt my feelings or play on my weaknesses. My dumpster hiding days were over.

Lesley Choyce, who has been teaching English and Creative Writing for over thirty years, is the author of dozens of books of literary fiction, short stories, poetry, creative nonfiction and young adult novels. He has won the Dartmouth Book Award, Atlantic Poetry Prize and Ann Connor Brimer Award. He has also been shortlisted for a Stephen Leacock Medal, White Pine Award, Hackmatack Award, Canadian Science Fiction and Fantasy Award and, most recently, a Governor General's Award. For more information, visit www.lesleychoyce.com.